MW01047808

Carson,
Keep on reading!

Chelsea
Fadden

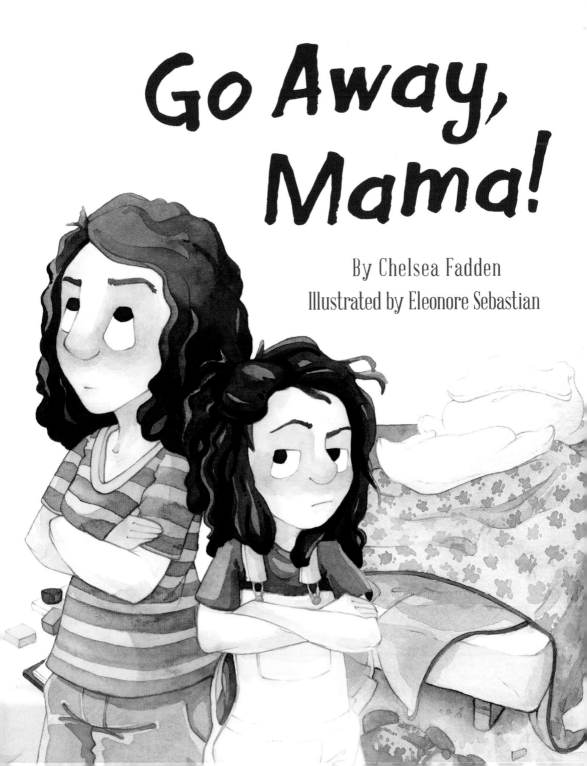

Go Away, Mama!

By Chelsea Fadden

Illustrated by Eleonore Sebastian

ISBN 13: 978-1-59298-678-1
Library of Congress Catalog Number: 2018945953
Printed in the United States of America
First Printing: 2018
22 21 20 19 18   5 4 3 2 1
Edited by Lily Coyle
Book design and typesetting by Laura Drew

www.chelseafadden.com

Beaver's Pond Press
7108 Ohms Lane
Edina, MN 55439-2129
(952) 829-8818
www.BeaversPondPress.com
To order, visit www.ItascaBooks.com
or call (800)-901-3480 ext.118. Reseller discounts available.

For Evelyn—I will always be there for you,
no matter what. I love you. Deuteronomy 31:8
—C.F.

For Mom—my biggest supporter and best friend.
Thank you for everything.
—E.S.

There once was a little girl
who drove her mama crazy.
She wouldn't eat her breakfast.
She refused to wear her shoes.

Her room was always a mess and
her hair was never combed.

It seemed her favorite thing to do was everything her mama told her not to do. When Mama said, "No," that little girl would pout and yell, **"GO AWAY, MAMA!"**

But Mama didn't answer with anger. She'd look her
little girl in those big brown eyes and say,
My darling girl, I will not go away.
No matter what, I'm here to stay.

The little girl grew. She grew until she was a teenager. She spent hours on the phone, wore strange clothes, and stayed up past her bedtime.

When Mom said, "Can we talk?" that teenage girl
would scowl and mumble, *"Go away, Mom."*

But Mom wouldn't yell. She'd look that
independent girl in the eye and say,
    My darling girl, you can't push me away.
        No matter what, I'm here to stay.

That teenage girl grew. She grew until it was time to leave for college.

And although she was excited to go, she was also scared to leave. She would be apart from her mom much longer than she'd ever been before.

When the time came for goodbyes, they hugged.
And cried. And hugged some more.

And before pulling away, Mom whispered softly in her ear,
My darling girl, I'm not far away.
No matter what, I'm here to stay.

That young college woman met a wonderful man and eventually became a wife.

Before long, that young wife was expecting a baby of her own. She couldn't wait for her mom to be a grandma, but she was also very nervous about this big change.

As she got ready for her new baby, Mom reminded her,

My darling girl, I'm still with you today.

No matter what, I'm here to stay.

And then that young wife became a mama.

As she rocked her new baby girl, she stared down at soft pink cheeks and delicate eyelashes. A fierce love washed over her and she finally understood. She held her baby tightly to her chest and whispered softly...

My darling girl, I will not go away.
No matter what, I'm here to stay.

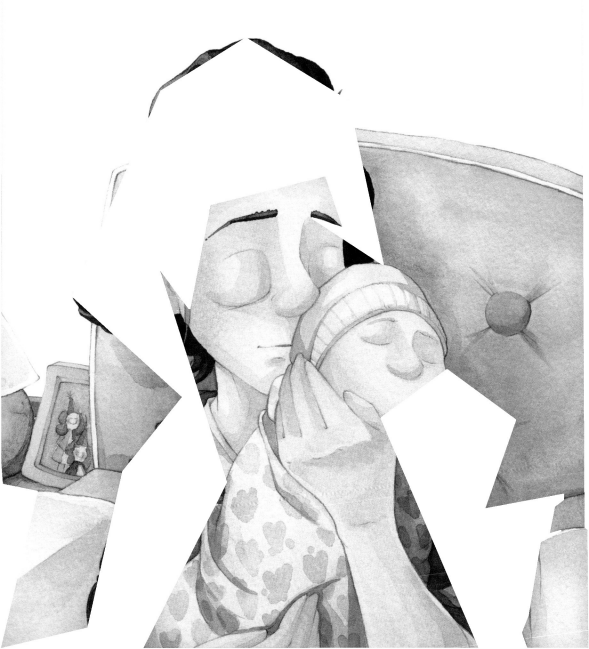

The End